STOMP, STOMP!

BY BOB KOLAR

North-South Books
New York · London

FOR LISA

Copyright © 1997 by Bob Kolar
All rights reserved. No part of this book may be reproduced
or utilized in any form or by any means, electronic or mechanical,
including photocopying, recording, or any information storage
and retrieval system, without permission in writing from the publisher.

Published in the United States by North-South Books Inc., New York.
Published simultaneously in Great Britain, Canada, Australia, and
New Zealand in 1997 by North-South Books, an imprint of
Nord-Süd Verlag AG, Gossau Zürich, Switzerland.

Library of Congress Cataloging-in-Publication Data is available.
A CIP catalogue record for this book is available from The British Library.

The artwork was created with watercolor dyes on Winsor & Newton paper.

ISBN 1-55858-632-6 (trade binding) 10 9 8 7 6 5 4 3 2 1
ISBN 1-55858-633-4 (library binding) 10 9 8 7 6 5 4 3 2 1
Printed in Belgium

For more information about our books, and the authors and artists
who create them, visit our web site: http://www.northsouth.com

**Hee,
hee.**

THUMP.

WHUMP!

Look at me!

STOMP, STOMP!

YA-HOO!

PLOP!

Whoop-de-do!

STOMP, STOMP!

TROUNCE!

STOMPITY-STOMP!

STOMPITY?

Oh,
my.

Bye-bye.